Ivanhoe

Ivanhoe

Retold and illustrated by
Andrew Skilleter

MACDONALD YOUNG BOOKS

For Molly, Owen and Eileen – A.S.

Text and illustrations copyright © 1997 Andrew Skilleter

First published in Great Britain in 1997 by
Macdonald Young Books
an imprint of Wayland Publishers Ltd
61 Western Road
Hove
East Sussex
BN3 1JD

Designed by Shireen Nathoo Design

Printed and bound in Portugal by Edições ASA

British Library Cataloguing in Publication Data available

ISBN: 0 7500 2406 2

Contents

Prologue   7

The Pilgrim   10

Tournament   17

The Disinherited Knight   22

Robin Hood   28

Castle   32

Inferno   38

Victory and Villainy   44

Lionheart   49

Witchcraft   53

Champion   57

Prologue

"Enough!" Cedric the Saxon's fist struck the table. "Rowena will marry Athelstane! As my ward she will do as I say. He's a descendant of Alfred the Great and she a Saxon princess of a noble line. What an alliance they will make!"

His father continued while Ivanhoe stared defiantly.

"It's been my life's ambition to bring about a new Saxon dynasty! All true Saxons will rally to the cause and overthrow the hated Norman tyrants! Athelstane and Rowena will reign as Saxon king and queen of all England!"

Ivanhoe could listen no longer.

"Madness, father! An old man's fantasy! I'm as proud as anyone of my Saxon blood but we can't go back a hundred years or more. We have a good king, Richard the Lionheart, who you will be defying. And have you thought of the danger you'll place Rowena in? Prince John and his Norman partners are hardly likely to sit back and allow a new Saxon alliance!"

Cedric simmered with rage as Ivanhoe passionately poured out his feelings.

"Rowena and I love each other. We've grown up together ever since you became her guardian and she came here to live at Rotherwood. She doesn't wish to marry anyone but me or be part of your mad schemes. And I will never accept her marrying another!"

Cedric gave out a fearsome roar thrusting his sword into the air!

"Then go! From this day on you are no longer any son of mine and, by Hengist, I disinherit you! Now leave – leave the manor of Rotherwood and never dare return while I live!"

Deeply wounded by his father's words, but still defiant, Ivanhoe strode from the room and into the arms of Rowena who had been listening at the door.

"Ivanhoe!" Rowena clutched at her lover desperately, tears streaming from her eyes. "I heard it all! How could he do this to you? What are we to do?"

Ivanhoe held her close. He felt numb, empty. "Dear Rowena, we can only wait and hope. I know my father – it would take the king himself to persuade him to swallow his pride and take back his words! I must leave for the Holy Land and join the crusades. I'll serve King Richard and prove myself a worthy knight. Do all you can to delay the marriage – I know you have the courage – and wait for me. Never lose faith – I promise I will return to marry you and claim my rightful place here, whatever it takes!"

The black-clad figure gripped his pilgrim's staff and looked up at the storm clouds that threatened the golden beauty of the sunset. He stood within a circle of ancient stones and stretching out an arm, greeted as an old friend the largest of them. Exploring its cold, rugged surface, his fingertips tingled with a curious warmth. Memories of his boyhood flooded back, recalling the moment he had first discovered an empathy with this great stone. Cernakus it was called and in thoughts and images it had 'spoken' to him.

Energy and light surged through the Pilgrim as his fingers remained rigid against the surface. A boiling cauldron of molten sound, light and colour sliced and ground his senses as visions unravelled before him until he saw himself in the Holy Land and then as the lonely figure of the Pilgrim leaving the stones. The future! He was going to be shown a glimpse of what was to come!

Great warhorses cannoned against each other, lance against shield, sword against steel. A black knight, a warrior of the woods, the suffocating density of forest, a terrible fire! The images flashed by at a blistering speed until a great red lion sprang into view and with a terrifying roar shattered the vision! The Pilgrim's fingers jerked free of the stone and he stood aware of a new strength and sense of destiny. He cast his eyes to the distant horizon greened by the vast forest of Sherwood where lay the dim outline of the Saxon Manor of Rotherwood, his destination. There would begin his great adventure!

The Pilgrim

The light was fading fast as a band of horsemen twisted and turned through the paths of the dark forest. As the windblown summer rain began to fall, the wooden outer defences of Rotherwood came into view. At the entrance, a grand knight, impatient for food and rest, blew loudly on his horn announcing their arrival.

Cedric the Saxon's strong old hands gripped the carved ends of his chair as the blast of the Templar's horn pierced the low hum in the banqueting hall. A hideous barking and yelping of the many dogs reached deafening levels. Cedric, fearing the worst, shot upright, blinking furiously.

"To the gates!" he cried. "Go and see what bad news that infernal horn brings. No doubt tales of robbery and worse on my lands!"

"The knight Sir Brian de Bois-Guilbert, Commander of the Order of the Knights Templar is at the gate, my lord, together with his retinue," announced the servant on his return. "They're on their way to the great tournament at Ashby-de-la-Zouch and request food and beds for the night!"

"Normans!" muttered Cedric. "This is a cursed evening, for sure." He hated everything Norman but soon his disgusted expression shifted to one of resignation. "Never let it be said that Cedric of Rotherwood does not look after his guests," he declared proudly. "Welcome them and see to all their needs."

As the guests gathered in the great hall for the start of the feast, the Lady Rowena viewed them with excited interest, especially Sir Brian, as he had only recently returned from the Crusades. He would have fresh news. Maybe even of Ivanhoe! Since his banishment, not a day had passed without her wondering how he was faring in the Holy Lands and when he would return. Not that she ever dared mention his name in Cedric's presence!

She sipped from the gold goblet remembering her first sight of Sir Brian's party. They were all Templars but surely there was one other who was not …? Of course, the young pilgrim! He'd met them on the road and had agreed to guide the group to Rotherwood. She looked around the hall and glimpsed the strange figure sitting alone by the fire.

Sir Brian feasted with great gusto, occasionally stopping to exchange words with his companions and Saxon hosts. He was unable to disguise his contempt for the Saxon ways and Cedric had to restrain himself on several occasions.

Power and too many bloody battles in the burning desert sun had blackened the heart of the Templar knight. He had begun fighting for God and the Templar order to protect the Holy places and visiting pilgrims. But now ambition, greed and cruelty ruled him, masking the emptiness within.

As his teeth sank into a succulent piece of pork he noticed out of the corner of his eye the arrival of another traveller. The thin, tall but stooping figure of an elderly Jewish man crept in, looking hopelessly for even the slightest welcome. Jewish citizens were disliked and were the victims of all kinds of injustice and prejudice. Having adopted the role of moneylenders, they were often cheated by Norman and Saxon alike.

Isaac of York! One of the richest moneylenders in the land! Sweet fortune smiles on me tonight. This is a lucky twist of fate but not, I fear, for him! Sir Brian thought, allowing himself a discreet chuckle. I'm in need of gold and I think he can be persuaded to part with some, on my terms of course!

The Pilgrim also noticed Isaac. Feeling sorry for the nervous figure he called out to him.

"Old man – over here! Sit down and I'll find you some food."

Leaving Isaac eating, the Pilgrim moved close to the main guests.

Rowena eyed the Templar knight coldly. Sir Brian was a commanding presence and there was no doubting his bravery. He was powerful too. Aside from his rank he was a close ally of Prince John. But he swaggered with a gross arrogance that repelled her. However, she was impatient for news and decided to turn the conversation to the Crusades. She smiled gently, her beautiful fair features betraying nothing of her dislike for the knight.

"Sir Brian, you must have news of interest from the Holy Land. Do tell us!"

Sir Brian looked up at her with his cold, dark eyes. "There's little to tell, my lady. We've secured a truce with the Saracen leader, Saladin, due largely to the might and discipline of our order. As you all know we have the best knights in Christendom and the enemy know it too!"

By Hereward, there he goes boasting again, she thought. Ivanhoe would be a match for any of his Templars. She boldly interrupted Sir Brian's boasting, her elegant expression veiling her irritation.

"Sir Brian," she enquired, "were not the Saxon knights of King Richard as brave as any of your Templar warriors?"

"Brave enough," he conceded. "Let's say they were second only to our Knights Templar."

"Second to NONE!"

A silence fell.

All eyes turned towards the figure of the young Pilgrim who stood, staff in hand like a venerable biblical prophet, his words demanding attention.

"I was there! King Richard and five of his Saxon knights held a tournament at Acre and they defeated all the Norman knights of the Temple who challenged them, including Sir Brian. I saw it all!"

Rage spread across Sir Brian's face. His shaking fingers briefly gripped his sword.

A dangerous moment passed.

"Name them! Name the five knights!" Cedric demanded gleefully, unable to disguise his joy at hearing of Normans defeated.

The Pilgrim named four of the five knights. "The fifth," he continued pausing briefly, "was a little known young knight. His name is of no importance."

"Then I shall name the knight, Sir Pilgrim!" growled Sir Brian scornfully. "Although the youngest, he showed greater combat skills than any of the other four. His name is Ivanhoe!"

Had at that moment a thunderbolt hit the roof of the great hall, it could not have surprised Rowena and Cedric more than the name of Ivanhoe! Rowena, flushed with emotion, just saved herself from speaking his name aloud.

Unaware of Ivanhoe's connection with the Manor of Rotherwood, Sir Brian continued, "I dare him to challenge me at the coming tournament at Ashby and then we'd see who was the better knight!"

The Pilgrim stood his ground, his face dark under the shadow of his brimmed hat. "Should he be in England, he'd take on the challenge, lance for lance, sword for sword!"

"If he doesn't, then I'll proclaim him a coward in every Temple court!" spat Sir Brian.

Rowena jumped to her feet. "Hear me! I too pledge my name that Ivanhoe would meet any challenge he knew of, especially yours Sir Brian!"

Torn between pride for his disinherited son, Ivanhoe, and dislike of the outbursts, Cedric brought his fist down hard upon the table. "I'll stand by the honour of Ivanhoe myself, so there it must rest!"

Rowena recovered her poise but her mind and body were consumed by excitement and anguish. "To have spoken his name … to hear it spoken … if only he were here …" she whispered under her breath.

Finally, well fed and tired, Cedric and his guests left the tables for their rooms and bed. The hall darkened and the smoke from the snuffed out candles and torches made ghosts of the departing figures.

Sir Brian beckoned two of his bodyguards to come near and began whispering. The Pilgrim moved closer to them, unseen in the dimming light.

"… and when that old rogue, Isaac of York, leaves in the morning, seize him and take him to Torquilstone Castle. I'll see if I can prise some gold from those greedy old hands of his!" With a cruel smile, Sir Brian dismissed his men and proceeded to his room.

The Pilgrim was grimly considering what he had overheard when the cheery voice of Wamba the jester interrupted his thoughts. "Sir Pilgrim! Would you honour this fool and share a midnight drink with me? You must surely have tales of great wonder from the Holy Land." Wamba, the son of Witless, and Cedric's favoured jester, looked imploringly at the shadowy-faced figure.

"Thanks, jester, I will."

Goblets in hand, the two figures sat close together, silhouetted by the dying embers of the fire and the light of a single candle.

"I tell you, Sir Pilgrim, my ears are still stinging from the boastful crowings of Sir Brian the Bore!"

The Pilgrim laughed and leaned towards the jester. "Wamba, as a trickster by trade, you know that sometimes all is not what it appears. Had you not found me, I was going to seek you out. I've a secret to tell you."

He whispered in Wamba's ear.

The effect was dramatic.

The sleepy jester somersaulted from his seat and would have shouted aloud with joy had not the Pilgrim urgently raised his finger to his lips. "Don't tell anyone what I've just said. Now listen carefully. At dawn unlock the main gate and fetch Isaac's mule and also one for me. Then come to my room. Remember – at dawn!"

The grinning Wamba nodded, his bells jangling merrily. "Your faithful fool will not fail you!"

⚜

As the first sunbeams of dawn entered through the window, the Pilgrim was woken by Wamba.

"Everything is ready as you asked," said the jovial clown.

"Good! Before we leave these are your instructions …" the Pilgrim continued in a whisper. "Now I must wake Isaac."

Startled out of his sleep by the Pilgrim's touch, the old man sat up. "Stay calm!" the Pilgrim spoke in an urgent hushed tone. "I'm here to help as your friend. Sir Brian's men have orders to kidnap you on your journey later this morning so we must leave at once while everyone is asleep."

"Holy Moses!" cried poor Isaac. "My life will be worth little in that villain's hands!"

Once outside the fortress, the Pilgrim and Isaac mounted their mules. "Farewell, Wamba!" the Pilgrim said quietly. "We'll meet again very soon. In the meantime stay out of Sir Brian's way."

"I may be witless but I'm a wise man when it comes to dodging Normans!" the jester replied.

He stood gazing after the two figures until they dissolved into the early morning mists. Clasping his hands together, he gave a little spin of delight.

"He's at last returned and disguised as a pilgrim! What a joke! Who can say what madness will follow when my master and the Lady Rowena discover that Ivanhoe has come home!"

Tournament

The two men had travelled some distance before Isaac broke the silence that embraced the forest. "I've made up my mind that I must reward you for saving me from Sir Brian's hands."

His confident tone caught Ivanhoe off guard. "I don't need any reward, Isaac of York. I'll leave the seeking of gold to such as the Templar."

"Very honourable. But you won't make much of an impression at the tournament riding on a mule with a wooden staff, Sir Knight!" retorted Isaac knowingly.

Ivanhoe drew his mule to a halt and stared at his companion. He saw in Isaac's face a wisdom he had not noticed before. "You called me 'Sir Knight' … are you some sort of sorcerer?"

"I've no special powers, more's the pity," replied Isaac. "When you woke me this morning I saw the glimpse of chain mail through the gaps in your cloak and I remember how you challenged Sir Brian in a way no pilgrim would've dared!"

Ivanhoe smiled wryly, impressed by his fellow traveller. Isaac continued, "I'll respect your desire to remain nameless but you're in great need of armour, weapons and a fine horse if you're to teach that arrogant Templar a lesson. Am I not right?"

"I can't deny it. You're a shrewd man, Isaac."

"Then allow me to provide them, Sir Knight! Let's travel together to Leicester. I'm to meet my daughter Rebecca there before going on to Ashby to do business at the tournament with Prince John!"

"I must accept," replied Ivanhoe, "but mark this. I'll repay all that you give as soon as I am able."

"Good! Good! May your lance be as powerful as the Rod of Moses!" responded Isaac jovially.

The tournament enclosure was set in a fine green field on the verge of a wood just outside the town of Ashby-de-la-Zouch. There was all the bustle and activity of a great market day with the added splendour of the knights' magnificent pavilions. Flags of all shapes and sizes danced in the wind, a confetti of carnival colour that dazzled the eye.

Rowena sat with Cedric in one of the luxurious galleries for those of high rank. It had been a long journey from Rotherwood but they were now well rested. At Cedric's invitation, her intended husband, Athelstane had joined them, much to her annoyance. What a dull man, she thought. Still, she had so far managed to persuade Cedric from making any formal announcement, helped considerably by Athelstane's indifference to her and Cedric's plan. But their appearance together here in the company of so many of the noble families and Prince John himself, made her very uneasy.

Her thoughts strayed to the warm refuge of her Ivanhoe. How she wished he could be here and challenge Sir Brian, and so melt Cedric's icy heart. Surely then Cedric would welcome Ivanhoe back as his beloved son and she could be with him once more.

The excitement of the crowd reached fever pitch as Prince John's cavalcade entered the arena. Having taken his seat, the prince signalled the herald to proclaim aloud the laws of the tournament.

The herald spoke clear and loud. "On this day, the five knights led by Sir Brian de Bois-Guilbert will fight all comers in single combat. The champion will receive a warhorse of matchless strength and the honour of choosing a Queen of Love and Beauty who will present the prize to the winner of tomorrow's tournament battle!"

To the accompaniment of wild music and drums, the five Norman knights, proudly led by Sir Brian, rode into the field, a pageant of magnificent armour and costume.

One by one the Saxon knights entered the lists, each challenging a Norman to single combat. Positioning themselves at opposite ends of the field, the first two knights faced each other.

The trumpeting of a fanfare seared the air and with a thunderous roar they hurled themselves at each other. Moments later, in the centre of the field, the lance of the Norman caught the shield of his challenger causing his horse to rear and unseating the unfortunate knight who crashed to the ground with a metallic thud. Despite some skilled jousting each Saxon knight met with defeat. Sir Brian and his Norman knights seemed invincible.

Despair crept into Cedric's very soul. "With each knight hurled to the ground, the honour of England is bruised yet further," he said sorrowfully to Rowena.

"Another challenger may yet appear. I've a feeling it's not all over yet," Rowena replied in an attempt to console her guardian.

The victorious knights strutted triumphantly, spurred on by further wild bursts of music.

Few people noticed the strange knight.

It was only the sound of a herald's single trumpet that turned the gaze of the audience towards him.

With his youthful elegance and the skill with which he managed his fine war-horse, he immediately won the admiration of the crowd. His identity was concealed

by his helmet while his shield and tunic displayed only the simple image of a young oak tree pulled up by its roots.

"There! A knight!" cried Rowena gripping Cedric's arm. "And look! He's challenging Sir Brian himself!"

From all sides came a collective cry of astonishment at his presumption. Sir Brian stood incredulous, just feet away from his challenger.

"Who are you, that wishes to throw your life away so quickly, Sir Knight?" he enquired sarcastically.

"For this tournament I'm to be known as the Disinherited Knight and I suggest you look to your own life rather than concern yourself with mine," the knight replied.

"Then take a last look at the sun, knightling, for by the end of the day there'll be earth 'tween you and it!" bellowed Sir Brian smarting from the Disinherited Knight's boldness.

With a fresh horse, a new shield and lance, Sir Brian surveyed his young opponent facing him at the other end of the field. With his slender build dwarfed by Sir Brian's bulk, the spectators saw little chance for the Disinherited Knight but that did not prevent them clapping, shouting and whistling in support of him.

The trumpets signalled.

The two knights tore towards each other like thunderbolts, their lances levelled.

The ground shook and turf flew into the air.

There was a sharp sickening splintering of wood as both lances split into slivers on impact with the shields. Each horse was forced back on to its rear legs, a cloud of dust obscuring the riders. It looked as if both would fall.

Saddle and horse pitched to the ground and with them Sir Brian was flung into the dust. The Templar only just managed to free himself from the stirrups before his horse raced away towards the edge of the field. The crowd roared.

Consumed with rage, Sir Brian staggered to his feet. He unsheathed his sword and faced his adversary who had sprung from his horse, blade in hand. Before they could come to blows the marshals of the field placed themselves between the two knights.

"Sir Knights! The rules of the day do not permit further combat. I ask you to sheath your weapons!" demanded one of the marshals.

Sir Brian slowly and reluctantly slid his sword into its scabbard. "There'll be another time, Sir Disinherited, when there will be no one to separate us. And then I shall cleave the flesh from your bones!"

The Disinherited Knight replied calmly, unshaken by Sir Brian's threat, "Wherever, whenever and with whatever weapons, I'll be ready, Templar."

The Disinherited Knight

The Disinherited Knight was the champion of the day! Accompanied by the applause of thousands, he was conducted towards the gallery of Prince John.

The stranger's refusal to remove his helmet fired the prince's curiosity. For one terrible moment a darkness crossed his soul. Could this be his brother, King Richard, returning in disguise? But he quickly regained his composure, realizing the knight before him was of too slender a build.

The noble warhorse was presented to the knight who acknowledged the prize with a deep, silent bow to the prince. He vaulted on to its back and paraded around the field to the delight of the exhilarated, cheering crowd.

At a signal from the prince, the Disinherited Knight turned his horse towards the throne and became as a statue, his lance pointing towards the ground.

"Sir Disinherited, it is your privilege to choose from amongst the fair ladies gathered here the Queen of Love and Beauty. Tomorrow, on the final day of this great tournament, it is she who will present this gold laurel crown to the knight I judge to be champion. Deliver it now to the lady of your choice. Raise your lance, Sir Knight!"

Gathering the crown in his hands, the prince placed it on the point of the lance.

"Who will he choose?" Rowena whispered excitedly. "There are so many noble ladies here of great beauty who would deserve the honour. And this mysterious knight could gain great advancement if he chooses well."

"Whether he chooses well or ill, by Hengist, he has warmed my heart today and protected England's pride!" enthused Cedric.

The Disinherited Knight paced slowly on his horse as if exercising his right to survey the fair faces, some feigning indifference, others more eager to be noticed, a few seeking to avoid his gaze.

He paused.

The spectators' anticipation increased and an audible murmuring circulated around the ground. He was beneath the gallery in which sat Rowena and Cedric. The knight remained still for a full minute. The audience was his alone. Faces flushed, people whispered, fingers pointed.

The tip of the lance bearing the crown swung slowly towards Rowena.

Nearer. Nearer still.

She needed all her powers of composure to retain her dignified expression. Her heart raced.

No! He could not mean her. Surely not. Impossible!

The crown fell gently, glistening gold, on to her lap.

With a great trumpeting, the heralds proclaimed the Lady Rowena the Queen of Beauty and Love! Cedric, joyful beyond his nature, proudly placed the coronet on her head to a huge roar from the crowd.

She rose with great nobility, her fair Saxon beauty now more radiant. Could anyone have read her heart, they would have known that never was a title more justly given.

The Disinherited Knight sat proudly on his prize warhorse, his lance held upright. Behind him was an imposing ensemble of Saxon knights, including Athelstane, which, as was his right as the victor of the previous day, he was to lead into battle against Sir Brian's equally numbered company.

It was the second day of the tournament and the ground was once again full, but none there had quite the heightened feelings of Rowena, enjoying her new status as Queen of the Day.

A trumpet fanfare launched the two forces. Lances lowered, they darted towards each other at full gallop, the Disinherited Knight a horse length in front of his companions.

His quivering lance struck home, flinging an opponent to the ground as the two groups met in the middle of the field with a deafening crescendo. Many fell to the torn turf. Some would never rise again.

The Disinherited Knight, his lance splintered, swung his mighty sword, a single, skilled blow to the helmet toppling another Norman knight.

The figures of the knights and their horses swirled like dervishes amongst the dust, their battle cries barely audible above the clash of steel. Stewards and squires ducked and dived in their efforts to remove from the field the wounded and the vanquished.

The conflict grew ever more ferocious, first one side then the other gaining the advantage. The trappings of chivalric combat were now defaced with dust and blood. The once noble field was now a cockpit of naked aggression.

"Fight on!" came the cry from one part of the crowd. "Death or Glory!" from another.

Sir Brian, his injured pride from the previous day's defeat fuelling a terrible anger, wheeled around his horse and with sword raised charged at the Disinherited.

"For the Temple. For the Temple!" he bawled.

Battling as he was with another, the Disinherited Knight was caught off guard. Sir Brian's great sword arched downwards. His opponent was saved only by the raising of his shield which almost shattered under the powerful blow. The two knights became as one, twisting, turning, parrying and striking, their heavy swords scything the air.

All other combat was forgotten as the onlookers shouted and screamed their fevered approval. Suddenly a general cry arose from the ground, "Look out, Sir Disinherited! Beware!"

Two Norman knights were almost upon him as the Disinherited, heeding the crowd's warning, struck a heavy departing blow on the Templar before turning his horse in order to escape his assailants.

His advantage was short-lived. All three knights fell upon him like wolves and it was only his great skills and the strength of his new warhorse that kept them at bay. He struck at this one, then the other. But the odds were too great. The Disinherited Knight was finished.

Almost.

He came out of nowhere, a strong and powerfully built knight in black armour on a huge black horse. "Disinherited! To the rescue!" the Black Knight bellowed triumphantly.

His first strike sent a Norman knight and horse to the ground, the sword breaking in the act. With a mighty wrench, he tore from the hand of the astounded second knight a battleaxe and delivered him such a blow that he too fell senseless on the field.

Leaving his leader to once again face Sir Brian alone, the Black Knight calmly turned and disappeared from view.

The Disinherited rushed at the bewildered Templar. There was a sparking collision of steel as Sir Brian's sword was struck from his hand, and in raising his shield above him, he lost his balance. His heavy body fell from his horse and ploughed through the slurried grass beneath. The Disinherited Knight stood over the mortified Templar. "Yield, Sir Brian!"

Fearing for the life of his Templar ally, Prince John stood up and raising his baton signalled that the tournament was at an end.

"Disinherited Knight," Prince John spoke loud for all to hear, "we name you champion of this tournament and give you the right to claim from the hands of the Queen of Love and Beauty the crown of honour which your valour justly deserves."

The knight bowed low but spoke no word. Trumpets shattered the silence and the crowd roared in salute to a great champion.

Rowena sat on her throne of honour. Beneath her on the lower step knelt the Disinherited Knight. With great elegance Rowena descended the steps. Respecting his desire for anonymity she was about to place the crown on the knight's helmet when the marshals stepped forward. "The crown must be placed on his bare head!" and so saying they removed the helmet.

Rowena gave a short gasp of surprise. Her head swam. "Ivanhoe! Ivanhoe!" She repeated his name under her breath before recovering herself.

Fleetingly he looked into her eyes. His tangled fair hair was plastered to the sweating, blood-streaked brow of his young handsome face. With gently trembling hands she placed on his head the champion's crown and spoke out for all to hear.

"Sir Knight, as champion I place upon you this crown of chivalry. Truly, I know no other who could be more worthy of this honour than you." The Disinherited Knight and the disinherited heart were reunited once more.

Ivanhoe kissed the hand of the one he loved, rose and with the aid of his squire left the field for his tent desiring only solitude and rest. Rowena, her heart full of joy and sadness, stood with a dumbfounded Cedric, watching after him and wondering what was to come.

⚜

"Were I to make a company laugh as well as you made all good English hearts swell, then I'd be the happiest fool in England!" said the jester once he was in the tent with Ivanhoe.

The tired knight smiled wanly. "Thanks, Wamba, you've done well. It must have taken all your wits to have excused yourself from my father's service and passed yourself off as my squire for these two days."

"As I've few wits to spare, I can't say how I did it!" grinned the jester.

Ivanhoe began to remove his armour as Wamba turned to gather fresh clothing.

There was a low groan. Wamba spun around.

Ivanhoe was swaying and then, in spectacular fashion, fell to the floor, where he lay motionless.

❧ Robin Hood ❧

A confusion of voices echoed within Ivanhoe's head. He prised open his eyes and, as if through smoked glass, saw a vision of dark beauty. Exotic scents weaved around him as slowly his sight cleared. A young woman was bending over him.

"See! He's come round," she said excitedly.

"Thank God!" said another.

Wamba pressed forward. "Master Ivanhoe! You gave this poor fool such a fright that had I been wearing my bells I swear they would have fallen off!"

"Where am I, Wamba, and who's this lady?" enquired Ivanhoe feebly.

"This is Rebecca, Isaac's daughter and you're in their tent at the tournament ground. When you collapsed I sought their help and we brought you here."

The familiar voice of Isaac interrupted. "Wamba did well, brave Ivanhoe. Rebecca is a gifted healer. There are many who have her to thank for their health."

"Sir Knight," said Rebecca, "I've attended to your wounds and fortunately none are serious. But you're exhausted and will need a good rest."

"And all your cares are looked after," Wamba added vigorously. "The bounty from your victories is secured and Isaac repaid!"

"My thanks to all of you. But I can't stay here, so where shall I rest?" Ivanhoe replied.

Rebecca smiled. "You'll travel with us to York where you can be cared for in our home."

"And I," said Wamba, "have consulted myself on the matter and persuaded my Lord Cedric to allow all three of you to accompany his party until the road for Rotherwood. You'll be safer as part of his larger group."

"With my father and Rowena? I can't do that! He is determined not to acknowledge me," protested Ivanhoe.

"Ah, but he won't know it's you!" continued Wamba. "He believes you're a sick relative accompanying Isaac. All that will be required is a little disguise!"

"And," added Isaac, "there are a number of vengeful knights out there who would welcome an opportunity to pick a fight with you! But don't fret, you can wear your suit of chain mail under your robe."

Ivanhoe grinned. "It seems, my friends, you've thought of everything."

"It's the least we can do. You saved my father and I'm for ever indebted to you," said Rebecca with an intensity that both surprised and touched Ivanhoe.

❧

The two men sat hunched in their chairs, their vulture black shadows stark on the table that separated them.

"It's agreed then. We seize them here!" He jabbed his rough finger at a point on a crudely-drawn map before them.

His companion nodded his head and smiled. "Then you'll have your lady and I that slippery rogue, Isaac of York, and his daughter. We leave Ashby castle in the morning!"

They came from all directions. Falling from the trees, leaping through the bushes, a blur of black and green. Dressed in forest colours, black masks hiding their faces, the armed men bore down on their prey.

"Outlaws!" cried Cedric who launched a spear with great ferocity, impaling an attacker to a tree. He went for his sword. Strong arms grasped the old warrior and dragged him from his horse.

With a sharp crack, Rowena's whip snaked towards one of her attackers, lashing him across the face and sending him reeling. Rough hands seized her as Wamba, his sword cavorting through the air, made a gallant but hopeless attempt at a rescue. Realizing his folly he tumbled from his horse and somersaulted into the bushes, making his escape. Already surrounded, Rebecca stood motionless with Isaac alongside the litter holding Ivanhoe. With Cedric taken and overwhelmed by fear, the remainder of the party surrendered themselves to their hooded assailants. It was all over.

Deep in the undergrowth Wamba sat sadly contemplating the fate of his beloved master and mistress. "What earthly use is freedom if I've no one to tell me what to do with it?" he said to himself.

A shadow fell across him.

Wamba jumped up and found himself face to face with a man of the forest. A bandit! Wamba stiffened but was relieved to see that the figure carrying a longbow wore no black mask.

"Relax clown, I come as a friend. I saw it all! Your master and his party are in no immediate danger. Your attackers were no outlaws of the forest – they're Normans and I've discovered where they are taking the prisoners!"

"So what can we do?" enquired Wamba, his imploring eyes betraying the glint of a tear.

"Cedric is the friend of all Saxons who seek justice so he'll not lack help. And we of the forest don't take kindly to being aped by a bunch of Normans. Take heart, jester, and come with me. We'll raise such a force that will make those impostors regret this day!"

"While you gather your men I'll gather my wits and fight alongside you. I'll show those cowards that a scorned clown can scatter smiles!" said Wamba, his spirits renewed.

His companion gave a broad grin. "Well spoken, jester! Now let's step out!"

"One moment," said Wamba, "can I ask your name?"

The forester continued to stride along the forest path. "My name? I'm Robin … Robin Hood."

❧ Castle ❧

Rowena sat alone. Around her the tapestries hung tattered and faded like her hopes and dreams. This once fine apartment was now her prison. She recalled how she had left Ashby castle with Cedric after the great tournament feast. Her journey towards Rotherwood had not been a happy one knowing that despite Ivanhoe's great victories Cedric still refused to acknowledge him. Where were Ivanhoe and Cedric now? And where was she and who were her captors? A burning anger rose within her. How dare they manhandle and imprison her in some godforsaken castle! "This Saxon princess is not for caging!" she cried and so saying marched towards the door.

There was the sound of heavy footsteps on cold stone outside. She froze. A key turned in the lock and the heavy wooden door swung open. Rowena eyed the finely costumed knight who entered. Maurice de Bracey! I remember him from the banquet at Ashby. A Norman knight close to Prince John! she thought to herself. With great courtesy he greeted her and invited her to sit.

"I'll stand, Sir Knight," she responded proudly, "until I am satisfied with the explanation you're about to give."

"Explanation?" he replied ironically. "Ah, that is simplicity itself, fair Rowena. I've chosen you as the queen of my heart and will honour you with the name De Bracey."

Fierce with indignation Rowena glared at the Norman. "Insolent knight! You speak to me as if there were some closeness between us, yet we've never met. No true knight would intrude upon an unprotected lady with such familiarity!"

Her sharp response grazed De Bracey's composure. Rowena continued, "And what of your cowardly conquest of an old man and this unfortunate lady? What sort of gallantry is that?"

"Proud lady, I am but a moth to the flame of your beauty and I intend to have you as my wife. I will not be dissuaded. As a Saxon maiden I'm doing you a great honour by offering my hand," De Bracey insisted.

"Fine words and foul deeds I say, Sir Knight!" retorted Rowena. "Believe me, when I marry it will be to one who respects my Saxon blood!"

De Bracey smiled like a cat with a cornered mouse. "Ah yes, perhaps you refer to King Richard's little lion cub, Ivanhoe? Dismiss him from your mind. I heard he left the tournament wounded. He can't help you now."

Rowena lowered her eyes as doubt began to crack her resolve.

"I tell you," De Bracey continued, "you'll never leave this castle unless it is as my wife! And remember, Cedric's fate will depend on your decision. I leave you to consider my proposal. Goodbye, my lady!" The door closed behind him.

"Villain! Rogue! He'll force no tears from me. I will triumph … I must!" she cried in anguish.

Half asleep, Ivanhoe's mind raced. The tournament battles unfolded and the image of the Black Knight loomed large. "Who is he? Where has he gone?" he muttered. Curiosity turned to sorrow as he thought of Cedric's continued rejection, then sorrow to love as the face of Rowena stirred his imagination. "Rowena!" Ivanhoe bolted upright. A dark figure moved towards him, her hand gently closing on his mouth.

"Ivanhoe, stay quiet!" He stared at Rebecca and the complete sequence of events unravelled before him. The journey, the ambush and then…? Rebecca took his hand, knowing he sought an explanation. "When we were captured it was clear they were not going to kill us so I gave you a mild sedative potion. It was vital they believed you were an invalid. I was about to wake you but it sounds as if another maiden has already done so." She smiled. A sad smile. In the short time she had known him she had grown close. From healing to caring to … loving? she thought.

Foolish feelings! What slightest interest could he have in her, a jewess! The anxious voice of Ivanhoe cut into her reflections.

"But what of Rowena and where are we?"

"Together with Cedric and my father, she's a prisoner in this terrible place!" Rebecca replied. "And Sir Brian plays some part in this evil game. Not content with persecuting my poor father, he's visited me a number of times – I fear he has some strange obsession for me! But I did learn where we are – this is Torquilstone Castle!"

Ivanhoe leapt out of his bed and peered intently through the iron grill of the only window in the simple room. "This is Torquilstone all right! I know it well. Sir Brian has us like flies in his web, but in catching me that Norman spider's trapped himself a hornet whose sting may prove his downfall!"

Wamba and Robin sprinted off the path into the cover of the bushes. They crouched, hardly moving. They listened intently as the dull, steady rhythm of the horse's hooves and the jangling of its bridle came ever nearer. Robin Hood drew an arrow from its pouch.

"You won't be needing that, Robin, he's a friend. It's the Black Knight!" said Wamba with delight, breaking cover. He tumbled towards the astonished knight, waving wildly and shouting at the top of his voice. "Sir Knight! I'm Wamba, Cedric the Saxon's jester and friend of Ivanhoe!"

The bizarre apparition of a colourful jester in the depths of the forest caused the Black Knight to come to a complete halt, speechless! A bolder voice then cut the clean forest air.

"And I'm Robin Hood, prince of this domain. As a friend of Ivanhoe, you are welcome!"

The knight replied heartily, "I see I'm amongst friends. Can you provide me with a supper and somewhere to rest tonight? I can see there's much to talk about."

At Robin Hood's encampment the Black Knight listened intently as he ate his supper. Wamba and Robin told of the ambush and the imprisonment, the knight's expression of seriousness turning to one of outrage. He put down his plate and rose to his feet.

"These tyrants cannot be allowed to succeed! I'll put all my expertise in the art of warfare and siege behind your cause. If they'll not release the prisoners then we must attack Torquilstone Castle itself!"

From the very edge of the forest came a single arrow arching through the air and embedding itself deep into a straw roof within the castle walls. The repeated blasts of the bugle pierced even the darkest recesses of Torquilstone. Its insistent demands brought together Sir Brian and De Bracey in the hall. An agitated soldier breathlessly presented them with a scroll of parchment. "Sires, this was wrapped around an arrow that was shot from outside the castle wall just minutes ago!"

Sir Brian roughly opened it and scowled. "Impudence! Peasants and thieves! See De Bracey, a bunch of outlaws demand that we release our prisoners within the next hour or they'll launch an attack!"

"Is it signed?" asked De Bracey disbelieving.

"Wamba the Witless, Robin Hood and the Black Knight. An unholy trio! Surely this is a nonsense!" concluded Sir Brian.

As if by way of an answer, a man-at-arms stumbled into the hall.

"Well fellow, what news?" demanded De Bracey.

"Several hundred armed men, sire – gathered just outside the woods!" he gasped, gathering his breath.

Sir Brian turned to De Bracey. "And we've scarcely enough men here to defend the castle! The best of ours are at York, curse our luck and we've little chance of sending for help now. Come De Bracey, we must organize the defences and quickly. I'll not yield to this rabble!"

Wamba looked about him. Steady streams of men were arriving from all directions in answer to Robin Hood's appeal for those who would fight for justice and freedom. Sturdy, strong men of land and town, their simple weapons forged with a fierce courage. More than two hundred fighters were already gathered on the edge of the forest, many of those skilled longbow men of Robin's own force. Soldiers and men in the service of Cedric had also been quick to arrive, eager to assist his rescue. Athelstane too had joined the Saxon force with his soldiers, having been shocked out of his usual apathy by the outrage.

Beneath the grey-green boughs of the old oak, stood Wamba together with Robin Hood, Friar Tuck and the Black Knight.

The knight spoke, his voice strong and firm. "No answer has been received from the castle and we can wait no longer. Their numbers are few and we are already many. With the help of your archers, Robin, a sudden attack will give us victory today!"

Robin looked thoughtfully at the knight. "I agree and you shall lead us. Forests are more our battleground than castles!"

Like razored rain the arrows fell on Torquilstone in their hundreds, sending its defenders scuttling and diving for their lives. Cloaked in the dark shadow of the forest's edge, Robin's men tilted their great longbows upwards. They drew back the strings, bending the supple wood of the bow and released their deadly arrows at the enemy.

The shrill cry of a bugle signalled the attack, the imposing figure of the Black Knight on his massive dark horse thundering forward towards the castle. Wamba, dressed as an outlaw, sprang from the forest with the men of Rotherwood together with Athelstane and his troops, while Robin bounded at the head of his force of fighters.

Up went the cry, "For Saint George and merry England!"

They ran through the grass, leapt over stone and rock, up and onwards! The blast of trumpets and the rolling of drums came from the castle as high on the walls the men-at-arms sought cover against the vicious shower of arrows. The men of Torquilstone knew that only the castle walls stood between them and the ferocity of the army that by every second grew nearer to them. They gripped their weapons, looked to the heavens and steeled themselves for the coming onslaught.

Inferno

Ivanhoe peered through the window grill. "The castle's under attack! Sir Brian and his men have overstepped the mark this time but they still have the advantage of the castle. We must find a way out of here and fast!"

"Here!" said Rebecca.

"An axe! But how …?"

"Your sword too! Wamba gave them to me before we left for home and I hid them in your stretcher," said Rebecca, smiling triumphantly.

Ivanhoe grinned. "Well done! But we've little time. This attack puts Rowena and the others in even more danger. See if we are guarded, Rebecca. Cry out!"

She did as she was asked. No footsteps, no clatter of keys, only the distant clamour of battle.

"Good! As I thought, they've needed every man to defend the walls. They'd hardly regard us as a great risk."

He gripped the small axe, striking blow after blow against the wooden door. Finally the splintered wood yielded to the blade and moments later Ivanhoe had his hand through the gap. He gave a whoop of delight. "The key's in the door! Just as I'd prayed it would be."

Ivanhoe stood at the top of the staircase, sword in hand. Rowena's image burnt into his mind and then blonde hair dissolved into black as her face merged with Rebecca's. An uneasy tremor went through him as he realized that his feelings towards the young jewess were more than those of mere gratitude.

He turned to Rebecca who waited by the broken door. "I don't want to leave you but for the sake of our loved ones, I must. I'll return for you as soon as I can – I promise!" Ivanhoe turned and then disappeared into the darkness of the stairwell.

Rebecca looked in anguish after him. "Take care Ivanhoe! Take care!"

With blistering speed, the attackers broke through the outer defences and began a concerted assault on the main gate. Crudely-made ladders fell against the castle walls, while surely aimed arrows allowed the defenders little opportunity to resist. The warriors swarmed up the ladders.

"Fire! Fire!" The cry rose above the battle, causing the Black Knight to look up. Yes! Wisps of grey-black smoke were rising from within the castle walls!

"By Saint George, the castle burns!" He raised his great battleaxe in the air. "On to victory, brave warriors!"

Ivanhoe bounded down the stone steps.

Another door, more stairs and then into a gloomy passage. He hesitated. Where would Rowena and the others be? Not the dungeons. Perhaps one of the apartments or maybe the old hall? Guide me, Cernakus, guide me!

Mad laughter and the stench of acrid smoke caused Ivanhoe to fling his back to the wall, his sword at the ready. Turning the corner towards him, her body swaying from side to side, came a demonic apparition, ghastly in the light of the smoking torch she held. A shiver travelled down his spine as he saw the eyes of a demented old woman fixed upon his.

"Burn! They'll all burn in hell! I, Ulrica the Saxon, have suffered a lifetime of enslavement in this cursed place and now I take my revenge!"

Ivanhoe stood his ground. "What in heaven's name have you done?"

"They thought my spirit broken but I've fired the fuel store and now the castle will burn!" Ulrica cackled.

"I'm here to free the prisoners. Tell me, where are they?" demanded Ivanhoe.

She became suddenly calm, her senses momentarily engaged by the authority of his voice. "The prisoners …? In the old hall … but the young woman, she … she was taken to the …"

"Where, for the sake of Hereward, where?" Ivanhoe yelled.

"The main apartment … north tower, but," Ulrica replied, already slipping back into madness, "it'll be too late. The flames flow fast and they are my sword, my dagger! They will purge this place of my tormentors!"

But Ivanhoe was no longer listening. He was running like the wind, the face of Rowena drawing him on and on.

He reached a landing with a large window overlooking a courtyard. He glanced out.

"Rowena," he breathed. There, not far below him, the princess was being hastily led by two men-at-arms towards a mounted knight.

Ivanhoe sprang from the window. His feet drove into the back of the first soldier pitching him face down on to the stone of the courtyard. His companion spun around only to be met by Ivanhoe's sword.

"Ivanhoe!" Rowena cried out in utter surprise. "Beware De Bracey!"
Seeing his advantage gone, De Bracey turned his horse and galloped off through a narrow archway.

Ivanhoe took Rowena's hand and pulled her into a doorway. He fleetingly held her, his face mirroring her surprise and emotions. "The castle is ablaze! We have to find Cedric!"

꧁❦꧂

The Black Knight swung his axe against the main doors of the castle. Such was the force and fury of the final blows that they splintered and fell before him.

Trapped between steel and fire, the demoralized enemy stood rooted to the ground. The Black Knight felled several at a blow. Their companions turned and ran for their lives as the Saxons that followed the knight surged through the gateway.

꧁❦꧂

Rowena and Ivanhoe ran through the cavernous castle towards the old hall. "Wamba!" Ivanhoe greeted with amazement his jester friend who stood before him with several of Cedric's men.

"Master Ivanhoe! My lady! By Hereward's ghost, you are both safe!"

"Yes, yes, but what of Cedric and the others?" pressed Ivanhoe.

"They're all safe," replied Wamba breathlessly. "Once through the gate I and a band of good Rotherwood men slipped into the castle. There were hardly more than a few guards in the whole place so we'd little trouble in releasing the prisoners once we found where they were!"

Ivanhoe and Rowena glanced at each other, smiling.

"What about Isaac?" enquired Rowena.

"Ah! We released him from the dungeons, unharmed but carrying on dreadfully about Rebecca!"

"Rebecca!" said Ivanhoe urgently. "You've not seen her?"

"No. I thought…?" Wamba stopped, his smile vanishing.

Concern spread across Ivanhoe's face. "Rowena, you understand – I must find her. Stay with Wamba and you'll be safe. Guard her with your life, brave clown, and wish me well!"

Touching Rowena's hand he was gone, heading in the direction of the tower where he and Rebecca had been imprisoned. As he pressed further on, the smoke thickened and the heat enveloped him. Beads of sweat appeared on his brow as he leapt up the steps fearing only for Rebecca's life!

The door was open and the room ablaze. "Rebecca! Rebecca!"

No answer came, just the mocking spit of fire and flame.

⁘

Sir Brian straddled his horse, the terrified Rebecca held tightly to him. "De Bracey!" he bellowed. "This is our last chance to get clear. Stay close to me and we'll head straight for the main gateway at a gallop! I'm for Templestowe."

"And I for Nottingham and vengeance!" replied De Bracey.

Furiously they charged the main gateway, scattering the few fighters who remained there still. Amongst them was Athelstane. He lunged clumsily at De Bracey, who caught him a crack on the head with a mace. The Saxon staggered and fell wounded to the ground.

The Normans were through!

Out of the castle, down the slope, thundering away from the burning castle!

With a molten rainbow of sparks and showers of scorching dust, hot stone and burning beams spewed to the ground as the first of the towers fell. The battle for Torquilstone was over.

Cedric, reunited with Rowena, sat, his head bowed, staring at the prone figure of his favoured Athelstane who lay, head bandaged and barely alive. Wamba and the Black Knight looked on. All the elation Cedric had felt at their rescue and the defeat of the Normans, drained from him as he saw his dreams for the Saxon dynasty fading before him. And what of Ivanhoe? He felt as proud as any father would of his son but while there was a chance Athelstane might recover he could not, would not, acknowledge Ivanhoe.

Rowena's eyes darted to Cedric and then to Wamba. "Ivanhoe hasn't returned. He must still be in the castle!"

"Ivanhoe?" said the Black Knight. "I'll seek him out!"

Well-protected in his armour and helmet, the valiant knight entered the castle. The smoke was thick as he made his way up a staircase. There before him, silhouetted against the fire, staggered Ivanhoe, coughing and spluttering, a rag clutched to his face.

The Black Knight lifted him off his feet and headed back down the stairs. A heavy, blazing beam gave way above them and fell with the sound of splintering oak. It caught the knight's shield with a massive blow. Only the Black Knight's immense strength prevented them from being thrust down the steps to their deaths.

Once Cedric had seen Ivanhoe was safe, he had left with the wounded Athelstane who was in urgent need of care. All eyes were on the flames that licked the summer evening sky. Rowena sat close to Ivanhoe as he lay recovering. "Victory is ours, Ivanhoe, but we must leave. The fire spreads by the minute!"

"But Rebecca …?" Ivanhoe looked away. "I failed her, Rowena … I failed."

"She lives!" answered Rowena. "Sir Brian escaped with her and De Bracey!"

"With Sir Brian! The coward. He's after a ransom or worse!" Ivanhoe replied bitterly. He'd abandoned Rebecca and when she needed his protection most he wasn't there. Ivanhoe hung his head, in his own eyes an unworthy and dishonoured knight.

Victory and Villainy

The torched castle enthralled the silent clusters of men that looked on. Abruptly the air was torn by the hideous wailings of a wild, manic shape that emerged on the top of a flaming turret. Like a blackened witch from hell, Ulrica swayed perilously, a scrawny arm thrusting upwards a fiery torch, her vengeful curses curling into the air. Before her grim audience she played the hideous spirit of the dying Torquilstone until the turret crumbled, plunging her to a fiery death below.

"Brave warriors, the castle of the Norman tyrants is destroyed!" the rich voice of Robin Hood rang out. "We'll all meet up at the trysting tree and in the morning share out the spoils from the castle. Torquilstone is no more!" As the weary bands trailed towards the forest, the castle became an inferno, a burning beacon of freedom and a symbol of hope to the oppressed.

"He will not, cannot, bring himself to change his mind even though Athelstane's badly wounded! Yet he turns a blind eye to our meeting." Rowena sat with Ivanhoe in the early morning light of the following day.

"My father is stubborn," Ivanhoe said solemnly, "but I will be reconciled with him somehow!"

"So we must part?" Rowena looked into his eyes intently.

"For a while," he sighed. "There's much to consider and the fate of Athelstane will play a part in this wretched game. Let's meet in the morning before you return with Cedric to Rotherwood."

As the blackened shell of the castle smouldered, all those who had taken part in its sacking gathered around the ancient oak. Many waited impatiently for the dividing of the pillage. Glinting in the pale light, silver plate, costly armour and fine weapons lay alongside a hoard of rich fabrics and other treasures. Such were the unwritten laws of Sherwood and the absolute authority of Robin Hood, all accepted whatever share was awarded.

"Robin, I need no share of the treasures," said Cedric. "I stay only to give my heartfelt thanks to you and your brave men for our rescue."

Robin smiled and firmly grasped Cedric's hand. The gentle tramp of horses announced the arrival of Rowena, serene and lovely in the golden light. All rose to receive her and, gracefully acknowledging their courtesy, she spoke.

"Bless you all! If any of you should ever hunger or thirst remember Rowena has food and drink. If ever you are forced from the forest, Rowena has forests of her own for you to roam as free men!"

Even the toughest man was touched by her words and they gave a great cheer, waving their hats and weapons above them.

"Goodbye, Robin," said Cedric. "I'm anxious to have Athelstane safely back at Rotherwood. He'll live but his recovery will be a long one." He turned to the Black Knight. "Sir Knight, you can't wander for ever. Please consider Rotherwood your home!"

"Thank you, brave Saxon, and I will indeed visit you shortly as I've a great favour to ask of you. But before then, will you lend me Wamba to be my companion and guide to Rotherwood?"

"It's done," Cedric replied, "and as to your favour, I grant it already whatever it might be!" And with final farewells, Cedric's party departed through the glade and melted into the lush green of the forest.

Under a tree, his head buried in his arms, Ivanhoe sat alone, sad and dejected. The fate of Rebecca still weighed heavily on his mind and he knew that the time would come when he must risk his life and happiness to save her. Isaac at least was safe but desolate on hearing of his daughter's abduction. The old man had set out for the great fortress of Templestowe, the headquarters of the Templar order. There he hoped he would find Rebecca and arrange a ransom for her release. As soon as he had news, he said, he'd send a messenger to Ivanhoe.

The cracking of twigs jolted the knight from his thoughts.

"Ivanhoe! Why so sad?" The Black Knight spoke to Ivanhoe as would a gentle father. "I leave soon with Wamba for Rotherwood and I wish you to travel with us."

"Rotherwood?" Ivanhoe rose to his feet. "I fear I'll receive no welcome there."

"For my sake come. Trust me!" replied the Black Knight.

"Then I'll follow shortly. Before I leave there's much to consider – Rowena, Rebecca, my future. I must be clear as to my way forward before I reach Rotherwood," said Ivanhoe. He shook the knight's hand warmly and they parted.

Ivanhoe slipped into a deep meditation. The recent past unravelled: his banishment from home, the adventures in the Holy Land, his return to England, all that had happened since. And, most of all, being with Rowena once more.

Like a sudden cloud over a sunny landscape, his mind darkened and the image of the stone circle slowly materialized. He saw the greatest monolith of them all, Cernakus. It "spoke" to him now just as it had done so many times before.

"Ivanhoe … the Blue seeks the Black … the Blue seeks the Black … Danger … Leave now … Now!" First the image of the helmeted Black Knight appeared on the stone, then that of a strange Blue Knight. It dissolved, a pure blue spreading across his mind. Ivanhoe opened his eyes, his heart pounding.

He jumped to his feet. "My friends are in terrible danger. I must ride like the Furies!"

The Black Knight and Wamba cantered at a leisurely pace through the forest, passing the time with witty talk and an occasional song. The jester, unable to keep still, performed a variety of comic antics on his horse. He sat backwards, sideways, on the horse's rump, then on its ears, while making countless zany faces for the amusement of his companion. His enthusiasm soon had the better of him and he tumbled on to the grass.

"It takes an artful ass to fall off a horse at this slow speed!" laughed Wamba, clambering back on to the animal.

They fell silent as they continued their journey. A while later Wamba drew himself alongside the knight and spoke to him quietly. "We've company and I don't think they are here to be amused by this clown. The bushes over there bear spears as well as thorns!"

With a speed that amazed even Wamba, the Black Knight spurred his warhorse

forward, tearing into the thicket and dispersing a group of the most heavily armed soldiers he had ever faced! For a split second he had the advantage as the first of them fell to his lance.

"Cowardly vermin! By Saint George you'll regret this day!" he cried.

Spears splintered against his armour and shield as he struck down one, then another. The others flung themselves at him from all sides but the very strength and determination of the Black Knight looked to win the day.

Then, crashing through the foliage from his hiding-place came a knight, all in blue, striking the Black Knight with such force that both man and horse were hurled into the mulch of the forest floor.

Wamba blew with all the breath he could muster on the horn given to him by Robin Hood. With the attackers momentarily distracted, Wamba leapt off his horse pulling his companion to his feet.

"Quickly Wamba!" roared the Black Knight, sword in hand. "Our backs to the oak!"

Stealthily, the remaining assailants moved forward. The Blue Knight turned his horse around. Behind his helmet, cold eyes hungrily anticipated a kill. He faced the Black Knight. Now he had him!

Lionheart

T he point of the lance pierced the chain-mail. With a strangulated cry, the Blue Knight fell dead, sprawled on the forest floor. His henchmen stared disbelievingly at the knight who had struck down their leader! Ivanhoe sprang from his horse, laying into the assassins. Nimbly he darted and dived, thrusting and cutting until all lay dead, their blood bringing an early autumn to the green leaves of summer.

Wamba and his companion knight smiled grimly at Ivanhoe. "Well timed, young Ivanhoe!" said the Black Knight, giving his deliverer a bear hug.

"Out of the blue and into the blue you might say!" added Wamba, never one to lose the opportunity to make a grisly jest.

"Now let's see who this strange knight is." Ivanhoe bent over the still, blue-clad figure and carefully removed the helmet.

"De Bracey! I'll shed no tears for him. He wasted no time in gathering his assassins, but why should he be so keen to kill you?"

The Black Knight looked down and said nothing.

Ivanhoe felt that this mysterious knight held some great secret. And soon it would be revealed – he knew it!

They turned as a band of outlaws strode into view and from behind them Robin Hood himself, grinning broadly! "We heard the horn but it would seem you need no help from us!"

"Robin!" exclaimed the Black Knight. "How come you were so close?"

"My lookouts caught sight of armed strangers and we set out after them," replied Robin.

The Black Knight placed his mailed hands on Robin's shoulders. "Robin of Sherwood, vanity has kept my secret for too long. Had it not been for Ivanhoe, I might even have taken it with me to my grave!" He loosened the straps of his helmet and lifted it from his head. Ivanhoe gazed intently at his sun-tanned, bearded face as the Black Knight undid the cords at the top of his tunic. He revealed one of three richly embroidered lions on the surcoat beneath.

"I am Richard, Lionheart of England, your king," he said quietly.

They all fell on their knees in amazement, dropping their weapons and baring their heads. Only Ivanhoe dared speak. "My king! This is a happy day for me and all England! I was such a fool not to have known it was you all along!"

"I set out to conceal my true identity so any fault is mine. And you, Ivanhoe,

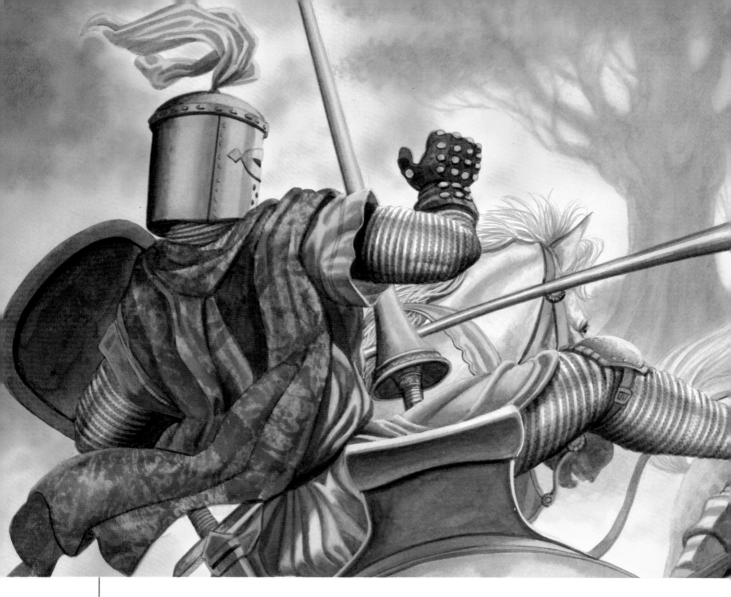

were one of the few who might have recognized my face, so in your company I was always careful to wear my helmet!" said Richard. "Now rise, all of you. I must thank you as your king for the services you have so boldly and unwittingly given me."

Ivanhoe paused thoughtfully, then spoke. "It would appear De Bracey was cleverer than I. He must have guessed the Black Knight was you, sire. And like many other treacherous and powerful men in this land he knew he could feather his nest more easily with you no longer king!"

"I believe that's so, Ivanhoe, but we've no time for talk. You and Wamba must accompany me. And Robin – I'll need these men of yours as protection. We ride for Rotherwood!"

His face set as stone, the Grand Master of the Templars observed with disdain the prostrate figure of Isaac who had been dragged before him. "You say you seek your daughter, Rebecca, and that she's been brought here, to Templestowe, by Sir Brian for ransom?"

Isaac trembled, not daring to reply.

"A jewess in our Temple? Your insolence knows no bounds!" The Grand Master turned to his deputy, Conrade. "You'll investigate this claim and report to me. In the meantime, lock up this Isaac of York!"

Conrade gathered himself for his interview with the Grand Master. It was not going to go down well at all. Sir Brian had been a fool! But he would present matters in such a way as to limit the damage.

"Sire, it is with deep regret that I must inform you that our brother, Sir Brian, does indeed hold a jewess, Rebecca by name, a prisoner here," Conrade deferentially addressed his leader. "But we all know of his bravery and his great work for the Temple. I can only say that I believe he has been bewitched by the woman and that she has him in her spell!"

The Grand Master was consumed by a superstitious outrage. He darted a fierce look at his deputy. "This is such an act of sacrilege and madness by Sir Brian that I can only believe you're right. We have a witch in our very midst! She shall stand trial and if proven guilty she must burn!"

Witchcraft

Rebecca started to her feet as Sir Brian entered the cell. "All's not gone as I planned. I'd intended you should stay at Templestowe in secret until the ransom was arranged. All would've been well if your fool of a father had not sought me out first!"

"What hypocrisy is this, Templar? What do you care of my fate, when you've done all you can to persecute me?" Rebecca replied fiercely.

Sir Brian looked away. "It's as strange to me as to you but I've come to care for your well-being. Maybe it's your beauty, perhaps your courage, or maybe you really have bewitched me!" He gave a nervous laugh and then turned once more to her.

"There's one last hope I can offer you. Should the judgement go against you, as it surely will, knowing Conrade, you can demand a champion to fight for your innocence. Under the rules of our order even the Grand Master can't deny you that. Farewell."

Conrade scowled and turned to his aide. "We must ensure that the charge of witchcraft be proved beyond any doubt. Then both the honour of Sir Brian and all of us remains intact!"

The aide cast a sly look at Conrade. "Rely on me. I'll encourage, shall we say, a host of witnesses to give such evidence against the girl that will damn her to the depths of hell!"

Conrade nodded. "Then see to it. The sooner this is settled the better!"

Rebecca, standing upright and composed, faced the austere figure of the Grand Master who sat in his elevated chair holding the symbolic staff of the Templar order. The entire assembly of preceptors, knights, attendants and scribes looked on.

The Grand Hall echoed to the charges of witchcraft. Indignation rose within Rebecca as her healing skills were presented to the court as malign magic. One by one, the witnesses testified against her. Poor wretches, mostly, who had benefited from her knowledge and kindness. Fearful of the powerful Templars, they told lies of magic potions and bizarre rituals.

A surviving soldier of Torquilstone was the last to testify. He gestured wildly, his expression one of wonder and fear. "At Torquilstone I saw her perched on the very edge of a turret. She raised her arms to the sky and then, may God help me, she turned into a white swan and flew three times around the castle! Then she settled again on the turret and became once more the figure you see before you!"

The assembly gasped as they greedily devoured the incredible tale, turning to each other and nodding grimly as if to say, "Witch!" "Guilty!" "Burn Her!"

Anyone with less strength would have crumpled before such terrible lies. But Rebecca held her counsel quietly.

The Grand Master spoke, "The charges have clearly been proven to us. What have you to say, Rebecca, daughter of Isaac of York?"

"I am innocent! The evidence has been falsely presented and mocks English justice! If you are to condemn me, then I demand a champion!" She tore a glove from her hand and flung it to the floor.

A tremor of shock spread through the assembly.

"So be it," said the Grand Master sombrely. "It is your right, but you must find a champion to appear at Templestowe before noon tomorrow. If you fail, or should he lose, then the sentence will be carried out. We'll allow Isaac of York to leave and search out a champion."

He turned. "And you, Sir Brian, as commander, shall fight our cause!"

Sir Brian bowed, his inner turmoil concealed beneath his joyless expression. He had brought her to this and now it was his duty to ensure she would burn!

With Rowena at his side and Wamba behind him, failing, as usual, to keep still or quiet, Cedric rose graciously from his chair to greet the Black Knight. "Brave knight, you are welcome!"

His guest raised his hand in greeting but said nothing. He threw off his cloak.
Cedric stood speechless as his eyes fell upon the royal coat of arms.

"King Richard!" The Saxon bowed low, followed by all those who looked on.

"At ease, old friend. On my return to England I wanted to roam free for a while and decided to play the part of the gallant in the guise of the mysterious Black Knight! You must allow your king his folly. But I'm here to have you honour the favour you granted me. Come forward, Ivanhoe!"

Rowena watched amazed as the young knight stepped into the hall greeting her and Cedric with a gentle bow of the head.

"Cedric, the time has come for you to make peace with Ivanhoe and welcome him back as your son and heir. I ask this as your king!"

In the presence of his king, Cedric realized that his plans to create a new Saxon dynasty were just an old man's dream. He could now banish his pride with dignity.

"My son, welcome, welcome home!"

Ivanhoe rushed forward. In his mind, doors that had remained closed for so long swept open, filling him with joy and light. "Father!" he said as they gripped each other tightly, reunited at last.

Rowena, her head held high, looked on in joy. She hardly dared to believe that the moment she had yearned for was at last unfolding before her. Tear-filled eyes and a trembling smile greeted Ivanhoe as they took each other in their arms and embraced.

"One further request, Cedric," said the smiling Richard.

"I know, I know, my king. You wish to see these two young people united in marriage," said Cedric enjoying his new role as benefactor. "I now see it was meant to be all along, by Hengist! Let all here witness I give my blessing for Ivanhoe and Rowena to be married!"

Spontaneous applause came from all those gathered in the hall followed by a resounding shout of, "God save King Richard!"

As Ivanhoe and Rowena sat together deep in conversation, their hands entwined, the dark shadow of Templestowe fell upon Rotherwood. A servant urgently whispered in Ivanhoe's ear and the knight left, returning to Rowena a few minutes later, his expression grave.

"Rowena, I'm sorry, but my honour as a knight means I must leave you for a while. If I stayed you would have a dishonoured knight for a husband. I'll explain everything soon." He kissed her warmly and swept out of the hall.

Though Richard was engaged in merry talk and enjoying a drink with Cedric, he soon noticed the sorrowful figure of Rowena. He beckoned to Cedric's steward.

"Find out where Ivanhoe is, at once!"

Bowing low, the breathless steward returned to the king with news. "My liege! He's left for Templestowe to meet Sir Brian in combat! Wamba has gone with him. Ivanhoe received a note from Isaac of York saying his daughter Rebecca is in peril of her life unless a champion could be found for her!"

"Ivanhoe in the midst of that Templar's hornets nest? Come Cedric, it's time they had a visit from their king. We must gather a force and follow him. To Templestowe!"

❧ Champion ❧

The insistent rhythm of the drums cavorted like angry devils in Rebecca's head. She sat ashen and still on a black-draped chair. The dark ugly stake with its fearsome manacles and chains jutted from the ground, imposing itself upon her. At its base lay the bundles of wood and straw. Here, Rebecca thought, she might burn. She closed her eyes and shivered.

Hours had passed.

Waiting, watching and being watched.

The scapegoat, the sacrificial lamb.

And still no champion. The drums ceased.

The Grand Master's voice rang out across the field, "It is time. We have observed the law and waited until noon. No champion has appeared." He turned towards Rebecca. "Prepare her for the burning!"

Strong arms lifted Rebecca and led her to the stake. There stood its hooded guardian, a blazing torch in his hand.

A trumpeting! The hands relaxed their grip on Rebecca.

A challenger had entered the field!

"Ivanhoe!" Rebecca cried aloud. Her new-found joy was quickly banished by a dreadful sense of guilt that it was she who had brought him into this new danger.

He rode slowly towards her and spoke loudly for all to hear, "Rebecca, do you accept me as your champion?"

"I do and gratefully. But I release you now, with all honour, from any obligation to me. If you must proceed then do so for the sake of truth and justice in this land!"

"I do so for you, Rebecca," said Ivanhoe. He turned his horse and with Sir Brian faced the throne of the Grand Master.

"Ivanhoe of Rotherwood, we accept you as the champion of the condemned. Prepare to do battle with our protector, Sir Brian de Bois Guilbert!"

"It would appear our fates are bound together," said Sir Brian, turning to his opponent.

"It may be so," replied Ivanhoe, "but today I've the nobler cause. While I fight for the life of an innocent and unprotected woman, you fight to see her burn. Dwell on that, proud Templar!"

The words stung Sir Brian's conscience. He fell silent and cantered to the other end of the field. The Grand Master raised his staff and threw on to the ground Rebecca's glove.

The two knights hurtled towards one another, their steel-tipped lances lowered.

"For the Temple!" roared Sir Brian. And Rebecca? his conscience whispered.

The impact of the Templar's lance lifted Ivanhoe from the saddle. Stunned, he felt himself falling with a heavy slowness to earth, all around him a darkening blur.

Rebecca raised a hand to her face and felt the coming fire.

Sir Brian vaulted from his horse, the white steel of his sword glowing in the midday sun. A vengeful thunderbolt, eager for a kill. But he slowed. His head ached with Ivanhoe's words: "… you fight to see her burn … burn!" He could see the flames, hear Rebecca's terrible screams.

His helmet gone, the sunlight streamed into Ivanhoe's eyes, jolting him from his stupor. His thoughts cleared. On to your feet! Draw your sword! He was bounding towards Sir Brian, who stood transfixed like a statue.

"Templar! Prepare to fight!" shouted Ivanhoe unwilling to take advantage of whatever possessed the grand knight.

Sir Brian appeared to awake from his torments. He lunged with his sword. Ivanhoe dodged nimbly, bringing his own sword down on Sir Brian. It struck hard on the Templar's shield. The onlookers gasped at the dazzling display of sword-play. Never were two knights so evenly matched!

But the haunted Sir Brian seemed to tire. His spirit was going from him.

Ivanhoe seized the moment. "By Cernakus, it is time to finish this!"

He leapt forward, smashing his shield against the Templar and with an immense swing, curled his sword against the knight's body. Sir Brian gave an agonized cry. His great bulk swayed and crashed backwards, sinking into the turf.

Ivanhoe's sword was at his throat. "Sir Brian, yield!"

But the proud knight could not reply. Destroyed as much by his own anguish as by Ivanhoe's sword, he would never ride any earthly path again.

Slowly the Grand Master rose. "Our defender is vanquished, God rest his soul. Under our solemn rules I must declare that the woman, Rebecca, is judged guiltless and may go free."

A malignant murmuring swept through the onlookers.

Rebecca took Ivanhoe's hand. "It's a noble act you've performed today. May all your years be happy ones with … with your Rowena!"

A tear fell from her eye. She loved this fair knight. There was no doubting that now. She must burn for him for the rest of her life, a fate as cruel as the one she had just escaped. Her life gained and lost at a single blow.

Rebecca was in her father's arms, allowing herself the flood of tears she had denied so long. Ivanhoe looked about him tensely, sensing the mood of the crowd.

"We must leave! Wamba has horses ready just outside the ground. Move slowly. I fear we're not popular amongst the more zealous of their company."

A sudden shudder of alarm shot through the assembly. Distant shouts, trumpets, the clatter of steel.

Figures ran here and there. Voices echoed around the ground.

At first inaudible, the cries became clearer.

"The king! Richard the Lionheart is here with a great army!"

Urgent glances were exchanged between the Templar knights as the Grand Master consulted his preceptors. Grim-faced guards gripped their weapons.

A sound like distant thunder came from beyond. Plumes of dust drifted into the air as the king's army came into view.

Richard sat proudly on his horse before the bowing figure of Ivanhoe and smiled admiringly. "It seems you've no need of your king, my friend." He glanced at the still body of Sir Brian. "But rise. I've assembled a strong force and all is in hand as you will see."

Richard turned to the Grand Master. "Enough of your scheming, sir! I intend to banish you and your meddling order from this land where you can do less harm!"

The Grand Master looked on with a poisonous resentment.

"Do not think you can resist me," said Richard. "Look! My royal standard already floats over your fortress. It is finished!"

Across the field came the colourful jester leading fresh horses.

"Wamba!" Ivanhoe warmly greeted his friend. "I think now is the time for you to play the fool and not the soldier!"

"This clown agrees. Better a weaver of wit than a wearer of weapons! And for all the colour of my costume," Wamba continued, thinking of Rowena, "you should be looking elsewhere for beauty!"

They both laughed. Ivanhoe turned to speak further with Rebecca but she was gone. She could bear to be with him no longer and had slipped away with Isaac.

Any sadness Ivanhoe felt at Rebecca's disappearance was overwhelmed by a glow of satisfaction. By saving her, his honour was restored. He had acquitted himself well, as a knight and as a man, and could now return to Rotherwood where Rowena eagerly awaited him. Ivanhoe and Wamba mounted their horses and, with a final farewell to King Richard, they set out on the journey home.

Cloaked against the cold, icy air Ivanhoe surveyed the landscape, its contours glazed by the pale, wintry sunlight. Behind him lay the age-old stone circle of some five thousand winters. Secure in their presence, he reflected on the year that was almost spent.

The late summer wedding seemed distant but Rowena was forever in his thoughts. Her retelling of Rebecca's visit still haunted him. She had come to ask Rowena to give him her heartfelt thanks and to leave them a box of jewels as a wedding present. He would never forget that dark beauty and hoped that somehow she would find happiness in the new land Isaac had chosen as their home. There, she told Rowena, they would be safe from persecution under the protection of friends.

He would have given them protection and Rowena had generously offered Rebecca her friendship. But she would not change her mind. Ivanhoe sighed sadly.

In the stillness, whispered words wrapped themselves around him. The great stone, Cernakus, addressed him in that uncanny way he had become used to from his earliest visits.

Ivanhoe was told of the great service he would give to King Richard and the royal favour he would enjoy. But also of times ahead when he would have to stand alone against the forces of evil.

He cast his eyes to the sky.

There before him lay a hazy vision of a great sword. He knew as it dissolved in front of his eyes that a strange and momentous adventure awaited him.

As the first light flakes of snow spiralled to earth, he turned to leave for the warm fires of home. And from the craggy face of Cernakus the ice melted and ran like warm tears into the snow.